Timmerman Was Here

Colleen Sydor

illustrated by Nicolas Debon

Tundra Books

Published in Canada by Tundra Books,
75 Sherbourne Street, Toronto, Ontario M5A 2P9

Published in the United States by Tundra Books of Northern New York,
P.O. Box 1030, Plattsburgh, New York 12901

Library of Congress Control Number: 2008909729

Library and Archives Canada Cataloguing in Publication

Sydor, Colleen
    Timmerman was here / Colleen Sydor ; illustrated by Nicolas Debon.

ISBN 978-0-88776-890-3

    I. Debon, Nicolas, 1968- II. Title.

PS8587.Y36T54 2009   jC813'.54   C2008-906648-0

ONTARIO ARTS COUNCIL
CONSEIL DES ARTS DE L'ONTARIO

We acknowledge the financial support of the Government of Canada through the Book Publishing Industry Development Program (BPIDP) and that of the Government of Ontario
through the Ontario Media Development Corporation's Ontario Book Initiative.
We further acknowledge the support of the Canada Council for the Arts and the Ontario
Arts Council for our publishing program.

The illustrations for this book were rendered in gouache, colored pencils, and wax pencils
Design: Leah Springate

Printed and bound in Canada

1 2 3 4 5 6   14 13 12 11 10 09

For Anne James,
who shines so bright and always will.
– C.S.

I had not intended to like Timmerman.
In fact, I was stubbornly determined *not* to.

Timmerman showed up on our doorstep exactly one week after Granddad moved out of our house to live in the senior citizens' home. Granddad said it was time he had the kinship of folks his own age, and some room to maneuver his wheelchair, and could I forgive him for going?

I said "Yes, I forgive you, Granddad."

But I wasn't about to forgive Timmerman. How could I excuse a stranger for moving into our house and taking up the space that Granddad used to fill?

I remember Timmerman standing there that first day, nervously fingering the rim of his hat. He asked Mother for temporary room and board in return for all the odd jobs she could send his way.

Times were hard, but I wanted to say "Not a chance! You don't belong." I knew Mother was thinking of our leaky roof, though. She was tired of setting out basins every time it rained. Me? I could easily have listened to the *ping-plop-patter* of raindrops in pots and pans for the rest of my life.

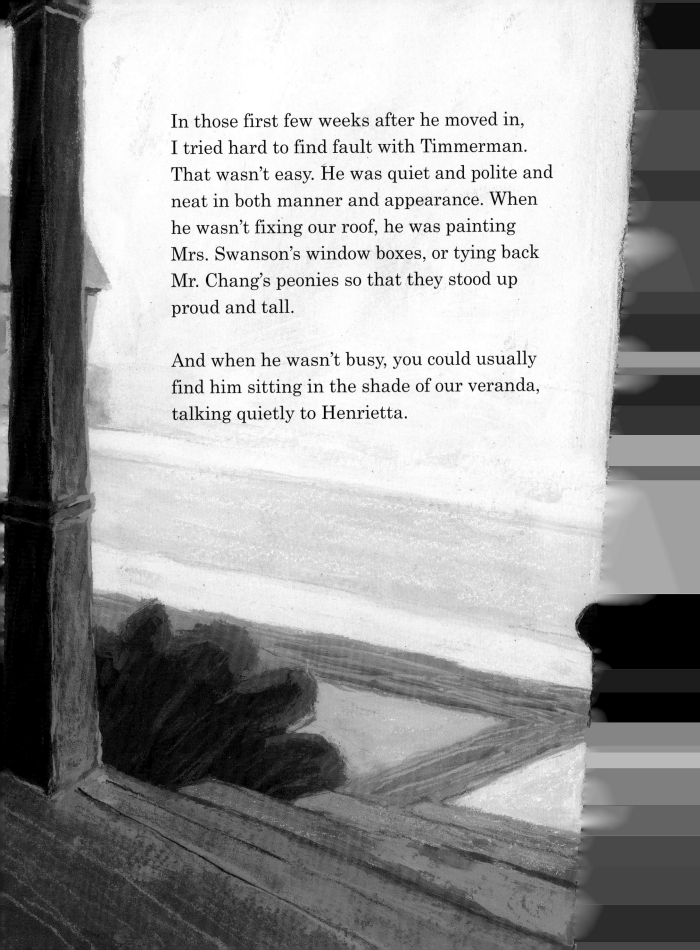

In those first few weeks after he moved in,
I tried hard to find fault with Timmerman.
That wasn't easy. He was quiet and polite and
neat in both manner and appearance. When
he wasn't fixing our roof, he was painting
Mrs. Swanson's window boxes, or tying back
Mr. Chang's peonies so that they stood up
proud and tall.

And when he wasn't busy, you could usually
find him sitting in the shade of our veranda,
talking quietly to Henrietta.

It was Timmerman's kindness to Henrietta that finally changed my mind. Henri doesn't take to just anyone – ask our mailman! But I watched one day as she allowed Timmerman to gently pull the burrs from her long, matted fur, singing softly to her all the while. Henrietta and I both had to admit then that we liked Timmerman.

What I didn't realize was that it wouldn't always be easy liking him. Especially after the gossip started.

It seems several of our neighbors had seen
Timmerman walking around late at night,
carrying a spade and an old burlap sack. It didn't
take long for the kids at school to fire up their
imaginations, and before I knew it, there were
rumors flying. Some said Timmerman was a
notorious bank robber who had come to town to
bury his loot. Others said he'd just gotten out of
prison and had come back to dig up the money
he had buried years earlier. And when Mrs.
Anderson's tabby went missing, they said it
wasn't money Timmerman had in his sack at all,
but dead cats.

If I'd been inclined, I could have added to those rumors. I'd often heard Timmerman leaving the house for late-night walks. But trouble sleeping isn't a crime. I knew he wouldn't hurt a fly, and I took a black eye at school for saying so. I wore that black eye like a badge. Timmerman was a good man, and it felt right to defend him.

At least it did until that terrible day I went looking for my lost book under his bed and found, instead, an old burlap sack and a spade caked in mud. The sight of that bag made me go cold inside. I thought about dead cats and stolen money. I looked in the mirror at the bruise around my eye that had only just started to fade. Suddenly, I wasn't sure about anything.

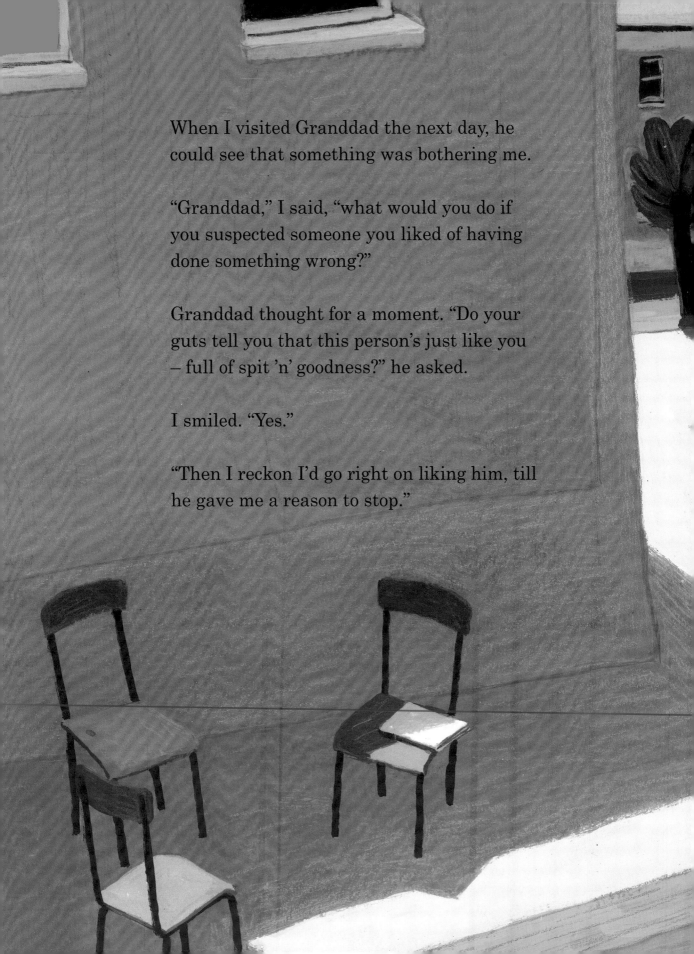

When I visited Granddad the next day, he could see that something was bothering me.

"Granddad," I said, "what would you do if you suspected someone you liked of having done something wrong?"

Granddad thought for a moment. "Do your guts tell you that this person's just like you – full of spit 'n' goodness?" he asked.

I smiled. "Yes."

"Then I reckon I'd go right on liking him, till he gave me a reason to stop."

Timmerman never did give me a reason to stop liking him. In fact, every day there seemed to be a new excuse to like him more. His way of including me in his jobs and accepting my help as if I were his equal made me glow. By the end of the summer, I was as handy with a hammer and nail as Timmerman himself.

Still, there came a day when I felt I needed to ask him about that burlap sack. "Timmerman . . ." I was nervous and stumbling with my words and he must have guessed what I was about to ask.

He hushed my lips with a fingertip. "One day you'll know," he whispered. "I promise."

Soon after that, Timmerman told Mother and me it was time for him to move on.

When he was gone, Granddad's bedroom stood sadly empty again.

I often sat in that room thinking of Timmerman, wondering about his old burlap sack. In the end, I came to realize that what was in the sack couldn't possibly be more important than the friendship we had shared. Even so, I got my answer.

For that spring, in a thick ring around our old oak tree and in Mrs. Swanson's window boxes and up and down Mr. Chang's sidewalk and in every yard on the entire street, sprouted hundreds and hundreds of colorful tulips. Of course, no one had planted a single tulip bulb. Mother and our neighbors could hardly believe their eyes.

Some said it was a freak of nature that brought the tulips to our street. Others said it was nothing short of a miracle. But I knew it was something much better than that.

I knew those tulips were whispering one thing, and they spelled out the words just as surely as letters carved into an old, park bench – *Timmerman was here!*